Best Wishes

The Invisible Boy

Sally Gardner

Sally Gardner is the author and illustrator of
The Fairy Catalogue, A Book of Princesses and other
popular books for children. She started out
as a designer of sets and costumes for the theatre.
She has a son and twin daughters and lives in London.

ALSO BY SALLY GARDNER

The Strongest Girl in the World
The Smallest Girl Ever
The Boy Who Could Fly
The Boy with the Magic Numbers
The Boy with the Lightning Feet

Lucy Willow

The Real Fairy Storybook (text by Georgie Adams)
A Book of Princesses
Playtime Rhymes
The Little Nut Tree
The Fairy Catalogue
Fairy Shopping
The Glass Heart

for older readers

I, Coriander
The Red Necklace

The Invisible Boy

Sally Gardner

Orion
Children's Books

To Dominic
with very happy memories of Splodge

First published in Great Britain in 2002
as a Dolphin Paperback
by Orion Children's Books
a division of the Orion Publishing Group Ltd
5 Upper St Martin's Lane,
London WC2H 9EA

13 15 17 19 20 18 16 14

A catalogue record for this book is available from the British Library.

ISBN 978 1 85881 840 5

Printed and bound in Great Britain by
Clays Ltd, St Ives plc

www.orionbooks.co.uk

"I can't believe it," said Mum, opening the gold envelope. "We won the top prize – a trip to the moon."

Dad, who was eating toast and reading the morning paper, said, "That's nice."

"Nice!" said Mum. "Charlie Ray, did you hear what I said? We have won a once-in-a-lifetime trip to the moon, all expenses paid, flying first class to Houston, then on the Star Shuttle, and staying in the Moon Safari Hotel, overlooking the Sea of Tranquillity. Oh Charlie, we are the first ones ever to have won this prize!"

Dad dropped his toast and paper.

"Let me see," he said. "Oh Lily my love, I don't believe it. We are going to the moon!"

Sam walked into the room to find his mum and dad dancing round the kitchen table and singing "Fly me to the moon and let me play among the stars."

"What's going on?" said Sam, who was only half awake and unused to seeing his parents singing quite so loudly on a Saturday morning.

They told him the good news, both excited and talking at once, so that it took quite some time before they realised that children under twelve weren't allowed. It meant quite simply that Sam couldn't go.

"Well, that's that," said Dad after Mum had phoned to double-check with Dream Maker Tours.

"I will be fine," said Sam bravely. "Look, you must go. It's only for two weeks and I have lots of friends I can go and stay with, like Billy. I'm sure his mum won't mind."

2

The great day arrived. Mum and Dad were packed and ready to go when the phone rang. It was Billy Brand's mother, who was terribly sorry to say that Billy was not at all well. The doctor had just come round and said he had a very infectious virus. Sam couldn't possibly stay with him now. Mrs Brand hoped it hadn't ruined their trip.

"What are we going to do?" said Mum, putting down the last of the suitcases.

"I don't know," said Dad.

Just then the doorbell rang. Dad answered it. He was surprised to find their next-door neighbour, Mrs Hilda Hardbottom, standing there.

"I just popped round to see if you wanted the plants watering while you were away," she said, smiling.

"That's very kind of you,

Mrs Hardbottom, but I don't think we will be going after all," said Dad.

"What?" said Hilda, walking uninvited into the hall and closing the front door behind her. "Not going on a once-in-a-lifetime trip to the moon! Why not?"

Mum felt a bit silly. She should have got this better organised. "Sam's friend's mum has just rung to say he's not at all well, so Sam can't go to stay there," she said.

"Oh dear," said Mrs Hardbottom. "Still, that shouldn't stop you. Anyway you can't cancel, not now, with the eyes of the world on you, so to speak."

"We really have no choice, I can't leave Sam alone," said Mum.

"We must phone Dream Maker Tours right away and tell them we can't go," said Dad.

"There is no need to cancel. If it comes to that I can look after Sam," said Mrs Hardbottom firmly.

Mum and Dad were lost for words. They felt somewhat embarrassed. Mr and Mrs Hardbottom were their neighbours, and had been for years, but they really knew nothing about them, except they kept to themselves and seemed nice enough.

It was Sam who broke the awkward silence.

"That's the answer, Dad," he said, trying to sound cheerful.

Mum and Dad looked at one another then at Sam. Oh, how they loved their little boy! It broke their hearts seeing him being so grown-up and courageous.

"It's very kind of you, Mrs Hardbottom, but…"

"Hilda," said Mrs Hardbottom, taking control of the situation. At that moment the doorbell rang. "No more buts," said Hilda, opening the front door as if it were her own house.

Plunket Road looked barely recognisable. It was full of wellwishers and TV cameras. Parked outside their front door was a white shining limousine waiting to take the Rays away.

A TV presenter with a games show face walked into the hall where Mum and Dad were standing. They both looked like a couple of startled rabbits caught in the headlights of an oncoming circus lorry.

"Mr and Mrs Ray, today is your day! You are Dream Maker's out-of-this-world winners!" said the presenter. "How does it feel?"

Dad and Mum appeared to be frozen to the spot.

"Yes," said the presenter, "I too would be lost for words if I was lucky enough to be going to the moon."

Hilda spoke up. "They are a little sad to be leaving their son. But he is going to be fine, me and Ernie are going to look after him."

The camera panned on to Sam's face.

"You must be his kind and devoted granny," said the presenter, pleased at least that someone in the family had a voice.

"No," said Hilda, "I am the next door neighbour."

The presenter beamed his most plastic smile and his teeth shone like a neon sign. "Now isn't that what neighbours are for!" he said, putting an arm round Hilda and Sam.

Hilda was in heaven at being seen by forty million viewers world-wide. Mum and Dad smiled weakly. Nothing was agreed. This was all moving too fast.

"I brought round a disposable camera," Hilda continued. "I was hoping that my dear friends Charlie and Lily would take some nice pictures of the Sea of Tranquillity, for my Ernie. He wants to know what watersports they have up there on the moon."

"Well, isn't this cosy," said the presenter, handing the camera to Mum. He was now moving Mum and Dad out of the house into a sea of flashing camera lights, and somewhere in amongst all the chaos that was whirling around them, they found themselves parted from Sam. The white limousine whisked them away. The last thing they could see was Sam waving bravely.

There were two things at the top of Hilda Hardbottom's wish list. They had been there for forty years and hadn't until today shown any sign of coming true. The first was to be on TV, the second was to be rich.

"I don't know what's come over you, sweetpea, you hate boys," said Ernie in a stage whisper after Sam had gone to bed. "You always said they smelt of old socks that had been chewed by a dog."

"There is no need to whisper, Ernie Hardbottom, unless I say whisper," she snapped back at him.

Sam, who was trying to get to sleep upstairs in the cold spare bedroom with no curtains, heard Hilda's voice, and crept to the top of the landing to see what was going on. What he heard made going to sleep even harder.

"Because, you numskull, how else was I ever going to star on TV?" said Hilda. "You have videotaped it, haven't you?"

"Yes, every minute of it, dearest," said Ernie.

"Good," said Hilda. Then she added as an afterthought, "Sam's parents must have taken out a lot of travel insurance, don't you think?"

"Well, if they haven't, Dream Maker Tours would have done, I imagine," said Ernie, pressing the play button on the video machine.

"Just think if anything were to go wrong with that Star Shuttle! Think of all that insurance money," said Hilda, rubbing her hands together with glee.

"That's not very nice," said Ernie.

"Who said anything about being nice," said Hilda, a wicked grin spreading across her face.

17

Sam went back to his cold lumpy bed. Tears welled up in his eyes. Oh, how he hoped that nothing would go wrong and that his mum and dad would soon be safely home!

The next day Sam went back to school and only had to be with Hilda and Ernie in the evening. All the evenings were long and dull. There was never enough to eat. After tea they would all sit together watching TV, and Hilda would hand out some of her homemade treacle toffee. The first night Sam had been so hungry that he had made the mistake of taking a piece. To his horror his mouth seemed to stick together so he could hardly swallow, let alone speak. All he could do was sit there trying to finish the treacle toffee while listening to Ernie snoring and Hilda's stomach gurgling like an old dishwasher.

Bedtime couldn't come soon enough. Every night Sam would thank the stars that it was one day nearer to his mum and dad coming home.

But then, on the day his parents were due to return to earth, the unthinkable happened. Houston said they had lost all contact with the Star Shuttle. They were hoping it was just computer failure. The slow, mournful hours passed and the Star Shuttle still couldn't be found. Finally a spokesman for Dream Maker Tours announced on the six o'clock news that the Star Shuttle was missing.

5

The next morning Sam got ready to go to school. He would tell his teachers that he couldn't stay with the Hardbottoms any longer. He had lots of friends at school. He was sure someone would help him while this terrible mess was sorted out.

Hilda must have known what he was planning, for she was waiting for him by the front door, wearing her iron face. "Where do you think you're off to?"

"School," said Sam.

"No you're not. It's out of the question. Not at this sad time," said Hilda firmly.

"I can't stay here, I mean I was only supposed to be with you until my mum and dad got home," said Sam.

"Well, they're not home, are they, so it looks as if you're stuck with us," Hilda said smugly.

"But..." said Sam.

"The buts will have to make their own toast," said Hilda, pushing him back upstairs into his room.

The next few days passed in a haze. Hilda didn't allow him to go to school, or even out of the house alone, not with all the press and TV camped in their front garden. Sam Ray's parents were a hot story. Sam's picture appeared on every TV, newspaper, and Internet site in the world. Sam just remembered flashing lights and Hilda and Ernie being called the nation's favourite neighbours.

After a nailbiting week had passed, the officials at Houston said the Star Shuttle had been lost in space. All on board were presumed dead.

That was that. No more exciting pictures to be had. The TV and pressmen packed up and left.

Sam and his parents became yesterday's story. Old newspapers blowing around with the dead autumn leaves, and like them a thing of the past.

6

Hilda had liked the idea of being the nation's favourite neighbour and had made the most of it. She wore a kind and caring face that made the press and friends of the Rays say Sam was lucky to have Mr and Mrs Hardbottom to look after him. Especially as there were no living relatives.

But behind the thin disguise, Hilda was making plans. She had rented a cheap bungalow by the sea and made Ernie write a letter to Sam's school saying that they were taking Sam away on holiday, so that he would have a chance to get over his sad loss.

Hilda's plan was simple, and that was to get her hands on the Rays' insurance money. She wouldn't be able to do that if Sam said he didn't want to stay with

them, and she couldn't keep him locked
up forever. No, the best thing was to get
right away. There were too many people
offering to help. Mr Jenkins, who had
mended Ernie's Ford Cortina, had said
only the other week that he and his
family would gladly look after Sam.

Ernie was a bit puzzled as to why Hilda
was so keen to keep him.

"Why are you going to all
the trouble and expense of
booking a seaside holiday?"
he asked. "We never go
away."

"Because we can't stay
here. People will begin to
ask questions," said Hilda
firmly.

"About what?" said
Ernie scratching his
head.

"About who is going to look after Sam," said Hilda beginning to lose her temper. "We don't want him saying he doesn't like it here."

"I'm sure he doesn't," said Ernie. "We can't look after him. We don't know anything about boys."

Hilda bristled like an old hairbrush. "I am only going to say this once more Ernie Hardbottom, and if it doesn't sink in to that sievelike brain of yours you can go and live in the potting shed with your CB radio for all I care."

Ernie looked at Hilda. She was not a pretty sight.

"The Rays," she said, talking to him as if he were five years old, "were insured for a lot of money by Dream Maker Tours, and now they are dead that money will go to Sam. Or to be more precise, to the guardians of Sam.

"If we play our cards right, that will be you and me."

"So we are going to adopt Sam," said Ernie, still not quite sure what Hilda was up to. "Don't you think, dearest, we are a little too old to be bringing up a boy?"

Hilda looked at Ernie as a cat might look at a mouse. "No," she said, "it means, you peabrain, that we are going to be rich."

"How do you make that out, sweetpea?" said Ernie, looking even more puzzled. "It's Sam's money, after all, and I don't think he would want to give it to us."

Hilda sighed. "I sometimes wonder how with a brain as small as yours you manage to keep going at all."

"That's not fair dearest," said Ernie in a small hurt voice.

"Oh, for pity's sake, life's not fair," said Hilda. "It is going to be our money and once we get our hands on it we are off to where the sun shines bright. Personally I am going to live the life I deserve. Sam can go whistle for his supper, and so can you if you don't buck up your ideas."

Ernie knew it was pointless to argue with Hilda. Once she got an idea in her head, it wasn't so much like watching a bull, rather a ten-ton lorry go through a china shop. Nothing was going to stop her.

7

That night Sam was unable to sleep. He looked out of his curtainless window at the back garden, with its neat rows of pumpkins, its potting shed, and its garden gnomes, lit up in the moonlight. He could even see the treehouse that Dad and he had made in his garden next door.

Sam flashed his torch up into the starry night sky. He had never felt more abandoned. Space seemed to him so everlastingly vast. Where did it end? He felt tiny and invisible.

Sam lay down and tried to get to sleep. Suddenly there was a loud crash outside. He sat up in bed. All was quiet in the house. Sam was sure that if it had been an important crash, Hilda and Ernie would be up in a flash, but nothing stirred. Sam looked out of the window again. Everything looked the same, except that something was glowing in the pumpkin patch.

Sam tiptoed past Hilda and Ernie's bedroom. The door was ajar and Hilda's snores were loud enough to cover the noise of the creaking stairs. He went down to the back door and managed with great difficulty to get it open. He felt somewhat stupid standing in the garden, in the middle of the night, in his slippers and pyjamas. If he was caught now he would be in big trouble.

He walked slowly down the garden path. There, among the gnomes and the prize pumpkins, was what looked like a metal salad washer. A little like the one Hilda used to clean lettuce in, but bigger and a lot fancier. Whirring sounds were coming from it.

Then, to his horror, a gust of wind blew the back door shut. He turned the handle, but it wouldn't budge. He was locked out.

Things were not looking good. This is most definitely a dream, thought Sam. For there, walking about bowing to the garden gnomes, was an alien with green and splodgy skin, saying, "Hello, I come in peas. Take me to your chef."

When the gnomes didn't reply, the little alien, who was only a bit bigger than them, adjusted the two long pink tufts that stuck out of the top of his head and started again. "Hello, I come in peas..."

"Can I help?" asked Sam.

8

The little alien looked up, not in the least bit put off by someone so much bigger than himself. "My name is Splodge," he said. "I am from Planet Ten Rings. I come in peas."

"Good to see you. I am Sam Ray," said Sam.

"Are you the big chef?" asked Splodge.

"No," said Sam, "I am just a boy. I don't cook."

Splodge looked at him and then said, "One milacue, please." He ran back to where the metal salad washer lay and went inside.

"If this is a dream," said Sam to himself, "then why does it all seem so real?"

"Chief," said the alien, coming out, "take me to your chief."

"If you mean Mrs Hilda Hardbottom," said Sam, "I don't think she would be too pleased to see you."

Splodge leant on a flowerpot and muttered to himself. Then, pointing to the garden gnomes, he said, "Who are all those people? Are they prisoners of the Bottom?"

"No," said Sam, "they are plastic, I think, and they don't talk. They are just there to decorate the garden."

Splodge started to make a funny noise and for one awful moment Sam thought he was choking. He was not up on alien first aid. Then, to his great relief, he realised Splodge was laughing. Sam began to laugh too. Splodge went over to where a gnome was standing and gently pushed him over. He started to laugh again.

"Ssh," said Sam, who didn't want Hilda and Ernie waking up. "Why are you here?" he asked.

Splodge looked at him as if he had asked about the silliest question going.

"Sauce of the tomato 57," he said.

This was crazy, thought Sam. "You mean tomato ketchup? You have travelled all this way for that?"

"Yes," said Splodge. "I have travelled from Planet Ten Rings to bring home sauce of tomato 57 for my mum as a present for her," he thought hard for a moment, "hello nice to see you day."

"Like a birthday," said Sam.

"What's that?" asked Splodge.

"Oh, you know, the day you were born," Sam said.

"That's it," said Splodge. "A birthday mum present."

"I think you might be in the wrong place," said Sam. "You need a supermarket." He pointed in the direction of the shops. "It's about a kilometre down the road."

Splodge bowed. "Thankyourbits," he said, walking back towards the metal salad washer.

"By the way, what's that?" asked Sam.

"A spaceship," said Splodge, disappearing inside. The door shut behind him. Sam waited, not quite knowing what to do. The spaceship started flashing with bright colours. There was an alarming whooshing sound as it started to rise. It hovered two metres off the ground and then crashed back down again. Another loud bang followed, the door slid open, and Splodge came out bottom first. The two tufts on the top of his head were now knotted together.

"Cubut flibnotted," he said.

Broken?" asked Sam.

The little alien nodded. "Whamdangled," he said sadly. "I need to make spaceship see-through."

"Do you mean invisible?" said Sam. "How can you do that?"

Suddenly a light went on in the house, and the curtains were pulled back to reveal Hilda and Ernie, lit up like figures in a toy theatre.

Splodge froze in fright. He had never seen such a scary sight before.

"That's the Bottoms hard?" he said.

"Yes," gulped Sam.

He looked down at Splodge, but to his surprise and alarm he had disappeared. Sam felt very scared, standing there all alone in the garden in the middle of the night in his dressing gown and slippers. How was he going to explain his way out of this one? His legs began to shake. Then to Sam's surprise he heard Splodge's voice.

"Hurry up," he said urgently, "it's invisible time."

"What?" said Sam. He couldn't see Splodge, but could feel something pulling on his pyjama bottoms.

"Hurry up," said Splodge again, "or you'll be whamdangled."

It was too late. The back door opened and there stood Ernie in his gumboots and Hilda in her rollers. She looked more frightening than any alien. She was flashing a torch round the garden. "I think it's that boy out there near the potting shed."

"Where?" said Ernie. "I can't see anything."

"That's because you are a short-sighted nincompoop," she hissed. "If that snivelling, smelly little toerag of a boy is out there he will be in big trouble."

"What are you doing?" said Splodge to Sam. "Now invisible time."

"I can't," said Sam desperately.

It was then that he felt Splodge press something onto his leg and the next thing he knew was that he was completely invisible, except for his slippers, which refused to disappear.

"I think you were seeing things," said Ernie, who just wanted to go back to his warm bed.

"I don't see things," said Hilda flatly. "Put your glasses on, and have a proper look.

Come on, I don't want to be standing out here all night."

"All right, all right," said Ernie, taking the torch from her. "Oh yes, I think I see something, sweetpea."

"What?" said Hilda, following Ernie.

Sam was frozen to the spot. His slippers seemed to shine out in the moonlight like a neon sign. Hilda and Ernie were moving straight towards him.

"I just..." started Sam.

Ernie looked round. "Did you say anything, dear?"

"Don't be daft, Ernie. Just keep walking," snapped Hilda.

It slowly began to dawn on Sam that he really was invisible and it wasn't his slippers that had caught Ernie's eye, it was the spaceship. Sam started to walk quickly back towards the open back door, his heart thumping so loud that he was sure that even if Hilda couldn't see him, she could hear him. He went into the house, Splodge still clinging on to his leg. Once he was safely inside, Sam shut and locked the back door.

10

Splodge stood in the kitchen tapping his foot. "See now you," he said impatiently to Sam, but all that could be seen of Sam were his dressing gown and slippers. Sam himself was completely invisible.

Sam was enjoying this and he was beginning to think that being invisible

might just be the answer to all his problems. He would now be able to escape from the Hardbottoms and get help. That was until he caught sight of himself in the hall mirror. There was nothing to see. How would anyone know he was Sam Ray if he was invisible?

Suddenly there was

a loud noise from behind him. Sam turned
round to see Splodge fiddling with a radio.
Sam quickly turned it off.

"Flibnotted! Fandangled! Need radio,"
said Splodge urgently, pulling one of his
tufts. "Must understand you better."

Hilda and Ernie were now banging
with all their might on the back door.

Sam picked up Splodge and went
upstairs to his room and got out his
Walkman. Splodge put one earpiece in
each tuft, then closed his eyes, folded his
arms over his fat little tummy and
listened. After a minute or two he started
singing at the top of his voice.

"Hip hop it never will stop,

This planet can rock the stars.
Hip hop this never will stop.
We are the men from Mars."

"Not so loud," said Sam desperately to
Splodge, who said, "Like the music, dude, it
rocks. So tell me, why don't you know
how to do visible-invisible? Do you have
learning difficulties?"

"No," said Sam, "we humans don't do
that." He was beginning to feel a little
worried. "What did you put on me in the
garden?" he said.

"My one and only patch," said Splodge.
"I was going to use it on my spaceship,
but when I saw the Bottom hard, and
you not doing anything to escape, I did
what any other Splodgerdite would have
done, helped you out. Because, my H
bean, you had gone and forgotten how to
go invisible."

"No," said Sam, "I keep telling you we

46

humans don't do invisible."

"How do you live?" said Splodge with great feeling, as if this was a design fault that should have been mastered years ago. "It must be something awful to be seen all the time."

"It is," said Sam.

"To a Splodgerdite," said Splodge, yawning, "being invisible is like moving leglot. It's just what we do."

"Sorry," said Sam, "you lost me."

Splodge lifted one of his little legs and pointed. "Leglot."

"You mean leg," said Sam.

"Yes," said Splodge. "It's

easy peasy, once you get the handangle of it. Like learning languages." He was now making himself a bed in Hilda's old sock basket. "Next day when the sun comes up to see you," he said sleepily, "I get my spaceship back."

"Will I be visible again tomorrow?" said Sam, but Splodge was fast asleep.

11

Sam woke to find he was quite normal again. He brushed his teeth, washed and got dressed, thinking all the time how wicked it would be if he was really invisible, and went downstairs for breakfast.

He was surprised to see that there were suitcases in the hall, and that Hilda was busy packing tins of food into boxes, which Ernie was taking out to the car. Perhaps, thought Sam, they were leaving and he would finally be able to get away. It was then that he noticed that the back door had a panel missing from it. He was about to ask how that had happened, but the look on Hilda's face told him it wouldn't be a good idea.

"Now listen to me," she said, loading Ernie up with another box. "We are taking you to the seaside for a few days for a holiday."

"I don't want to go, I can't go," said Sam, feeling panicky. "I mean I don't want to leave my house, in case my mum and dad get back and can't find me."

"He's got a point, lambkin," said Ernie resting the box on the edge of the kitchen table. "Anyway, who's going to water my prize pumpkins?"

"You keep out of this, Ernie Hardbottom," said Hilda firmly. "Now you listen to me, young man. Your mum and dad are not coming back ever. The sooner you get that into your head the better."

Sam could feel tears burning at the back of his eyes.

"You should be grateful," said Hilda, picking up the metal salad washer and putting it on top of the box Ernie was carrying, "that we are going to all this trouble just for you."

"There's no need," said Sam desperately. "Why don't you go, and I can stay with a friend?"

Hilda's face twisted into that of a witch.

Sam wasn't going to cry in front of her. He looked again at the metal salad washer. He was sure he had seen it before.

"Where did you get this?" he asked, picking it up.

Hilda snatched it from him. "Stop fiddling, and get out of here before I box your ears, you ungrateful little scallywag." It was then that she let out a small scream. "What have you done to your ear?"

"Nothing," said Sam.

"Shouldn't boys have two ears, dearest?" said Ernie.

"Of course they should, peabrain." She pulled Sam over to the mirror. Sure enough one of his ears was invisible, although he could still feel it.

"Perhaps it fell off," said Ernie. "I think we'd better start looking for it, and then take him to the hospital to see if they can stick it back again."

"Shut up, Ernie, and take that box out to the car," said Hilda, looking at Sam carefully. "Are you playing games with me?" she said, reaching out to touch the missing ear. Sam moved away fast.

"I think Ernie's right, we should stay here," said Sam.

"Oh you do, do you?" said Hilda, folding her arms over her ample chest. "Well, I'm not fooled by your little joke. Now get upstairs and pack, and by the way, if you see your missing ear bring it with you."

12

Sam's only comforting
thought was that perhaps it
wasn't a dream, in which case he should
find an alien called Splodge sleeping in the
sewing basket. To his delight and great
relief, there he was, curled up into a ball.

"Good moon to you," said Splodge,
stretching out his little arms.

"We're off, come down here now,"
shouted Hilda.

"Is that the call of the Bottom hard?"
asked Splodge sleepily.

"Look," said Sam, "I don't want to go,
but they are taking me to the seaside and
I can't leave you here all alone."

"I can't leave my spaceship," said
Splodge, "so I suppose this is toodleoo."

"Then I've got bad news," said Sam. "It's
packed in the car that's taking me away.

Hilda thinks it's a salad washer."

Splodge sat up and looked at Sam. "That's a first rate spaceship," he said.

Hilda's voice had got louder and nastier. "If I have to come up and get you, there will be big trouble. Do you hear me, boy?"

Without another word Splodge got up, made his way over to the rucksack and climbed in. "The one good thing is that you're visible again," he said, making himself comfortable.

"Apart from one ear," said Sam, picking up his rucksack.

"What's an ear between aliens?" said
Splodge.

The Ford Cortina was packed to
bursting. Ernie was so small that he had to
sit on three cushions before he could see
over the wheel. Sam wondered why Hilda
didn't drive, as she was the one that gave
all the instructions.

"You are going too fast, keep over to
the left, no you shouldn't be in that gear."

All Ernie would say was a feeble, "Yes
dear, no dear."

It took the best part of a day to get to
Skipton-on-Sea and when they finally
arrived, smoke was coming out of the

bonnet of the car. It came to a grinding halt outside a dismal-looking bungalow that smelt of damp and was colder inside than it was out. Why anyone would come here for a holiday was beyond Sam. His heart sank.

"This will do very nicely," said Hilda.

"Well," said Ernie, "the sea air must agree with our Sam because look, sweetpea, his ear is back again."

"Of course it is," snapped Hilda. "It was only that smelly little toerag's idea of a joke and I don't laugh that easily."

"No," said Ernie, "no, you don't."

13

It was hard to imagine a more miserable and isolated place. Even when tea was made and the lights turned on it had the feeling of being at the end of the world, and there was no way back.

Sam's room was smaller than the last one, and worst of all, the walls seemed to be made of paper. He could hear every word of what Hilda and Ernie had to say and none of it was good. Finally he could hear Hilda snoring, and he knew he was safe to look in his rucksack. He wanted to make sure he hadn't gone completely mad that morning imagining an alien, and a spaceship that looked like a salad washer. It was the only thing that had given him hope, as they drove farther and farther away from his home, from all that he knew and loved.

Sam emptied his rucksack carefully. There was no Splodge. He must have imagined it. He looked again. There were only the few things he had packed this morning. He turned it inside out. Tears started to roll down his face. He should have run away before they kidnapped him. Now Sam was lost just like his mum and dad.

He was lying in bed wondering, if he ran away, would he be able to find his way back, when the bedroom door opened all by itself.

Sam sat up in bed and flashed his torch. There, slowly making its way across the floor, without anyone helping it, was a bottle of tomato ketchup.

It came to a stop, and then Sam heard the padding of little feet and saw a plate of finger-size sandwiches wobbling in the air. They tottered one way, then another. Sam shone his torch on to the plate. A small voice said, "Stop it, I can't see."

"Is that you, Splodge?" said Sam hopefully.

"Who else," said Splodge, becoming visible again, with the plate of sandwiches in his hands. Sam had never been so pleased to see an alien before.

"These," said Splodge proudly, "are for you. Sandwiches of tomato ketchup and pea butter with nut."

Sam was so hungry that he ate them all down. They tasted great.

"Good news," said Splodge, "I have found my spaceship. Bad bit, wet inside."

"That's because Hilda thinks it's a salad washer," said Sam.

"It's a Viszler Junior Space Carrier," said

Splodge, sounding offended, "and that monster alien thinks it's a salad washer, whatever that may be."

"It's something you put lettuce in and then you whizz it around and hey presto you have clean lettuce," said Sam, finishing the last of the sandwiches.

"Or hay pisboo you have a broken spaceship," said Splodge.

"I'm sorry," said Sam.

Splodge didn't look up. He was busy, comforting himself by sucking the tomato ketchup out of the bottle.

14

For the first time since coming to stay with the Hardbottoms, Sam didn't feel alone. He sat on the bed with Splodge, looking out of the window. The moon looked like a big balloon that had come to rest on the garden wall.

Sam told Splodge about his parents' disastrous trip and how everyone thought they were dead and lost in space.

Splodge tutted. "I shouldn't think so, they most probably got stuck inside a grotter. Has anybody gone and looked?"

"What's that?" asked Sam.

"Surely you know what a grotter is," said Splodge.

"No I don't," said Sam. "I haven't a clue, what is it?"

Splodge looked worried. "Don't you learn anything at school then?"

"Maths, English, and history, mainly boring things like that," said Sam.

"Not about the planets, and the stars, and space dragons?" said Splodge. "Or how to look after a grotter, and what to do if an orgback turns up?"

"No," said Sam, who thought he would much rather learn about space than William the Conqueror.

"Grotters," continued Splodge, "are black as space and hard to see. They have huge tum tums and float about with their mouths wide open feeding on metricels of light, gaggerling up whatever gets in their way."

Sam looked at Splodge, still not understanding what he was talking about.

"Planet Ten Rings," explained Splodge," is milacue. So we look after the grotters and they look after us. Keep the orgbacks away, for a start."

"What are they?" said Sam.

"Humungous space monsters that can gaggerly up whole stars," said Splodge.

"Why don't you think an orgback swallowed the Star Shuttle then?" said Sam.

"Not possible, they live deep in space and we hardly ever see them. They wouldn't be bothered with a smidger of a thing like a spaceship. It wouldn't be worth munching."

"Would a Star Shuttle be all right inside a grotter or would that be the end of it?" asked Sam anxiously.

"More likely to make a grotter tum feel all wobbly and wonky," said Splodge. "I need to get a message home to my mum and dad. Then I would be able to tell them about the Star Shuttle."

But the problem was, how were they going to do that, now Splodge's spaceship was broken.

15

The morning did not bring with it a cheerful picture of holiday bliss. Thin drizzle fell and Sam could not see the sea because of a cement wall that blocked out the view. All the neighbouring bungalows were boarded up.

Hilda was busy trying to sort out the kitchen. "Did you get up in the night and take some food?" she said in a menacing voice.

"No," said Sam.

"Well, there are breadcrumbs where breadcrumbs shouldn't be," said Hilda.

"Perhaps there's mice," said Sam.

Hilda picked up the broom and shook it at Sam. "I don't want any more of your cheek, you little toerag. Go out and play."

"It's raining," said Sam.

"Out!" shouted Hilda.

Sam went out into the back yard. You couldn't call it a garden. It had high walls and crazy paving, and looked more like a prison yard. In it were two broken garden chairs, a washing line with a mouldy dishcloth hanging from it, and a pot with some tired plastic flowers sticking out of it.

Ernie was in the tiny shed at the back, fiddling about with wires.

"What are you doing?" asked Sam.

Ernie nearly jumped out of his skin. "Nothing, dear, nothing," he said. "Oh, it's you. What do you want?"

"It's raining," said Sam.

"Oh all right, you can stay here, but don't fiddle," said Ernie.

"What's that?" asked Sam, pointing to a funny-looking machine.

"It's a citizen's band radio," said Ernie, beaming with pride as he showed Sam how it worked. "It's not like your everyday radio. Before I retired I used to drive long distance lorries, and this is how we talked to each other. We all had different names." Ernie blushed and said, "I was called Tiger Raw. Sometimes if I was lucky, I would be able to pick up signals on it from as far away as Russia and beyond. Isn't she beautiful!"

"Could it send messages into space?" asked Sam eagerly.

"I don't rightly know," said Ernie, scratching the top of his head. "That's a mighty long way away, isn't it. I mean, it's farther than Russia."

"Only a little bit," said Sam.

"Anyway, I've just bought a bigger receiver," said Ernie, "but I'm having trouble wiring it up. The instructions seem to be written in double Dutch," he said sadly, looking at the manual.

"Ernie, where are you?" shouted Hilda.

"Out here, sweetpea," called Ernie.

"What are you doing?"

"Nothing, dearest, just fiddling," said Ernie.

"Stop it right now," shouted Hilda, "and come in here and help me make pea soup. And you too," Hilda shouted at Sam.

An awful smell of overcooked vegetables greeted them as they walked into the kitchen.

"I want you to stir this," said Hilda, showing Sam a pot of smelly, slimy green liquid. "Don't let it stick to the bottom. That soup is going to have to last us a week."

Sam sighed, and did as he was told. It was then that he realised both his hands were going invisible.

"Hilda," said Ernie, staring at Sam, "do you think boys fade away when they are unhappy?"

"What gibberish are you talking now, Ernie?" said Hilda.

"Sam's hands. They've gone and vanished," said Ernie.

Hilda turned on Sam. "You are doing this on purpose, aren't you, you ungrateful boy, and after all the trouble that we've gone to!"

"I just want to go home," said Sam bravely. "I shouldn't be here."

"He's got a point, dearest," said Ernie.

Hilda looked more frightening than an old flesh-eating dinosaur, all red and furious. "You keep out of this, you peabrain," she snapped, towering over Sam. "You'd better stay in your room until you learn not to play any more of these jokes, or you'll be sorry you were ever born."

16

Splodge was on the bed, listening to Sam's Walkman, and finishing off the last of the tomato ketchup.

"The good news," said Sam, sitting down next to him, "is that Ernie has a radio and a powerful receiver which he can't work. It just might get a message back to your planet. The bad news is, I'm grounded until my hands become visible again."

"It's going to be a long time then," said Splodge.

Sam was slowly fading away. By teatime he was completely invisible. All that could be seen of him were his clothes.

"I don't think I should have stuck that patch on you, " said Splodge anxiously. "It was meant for spacecraft, not for H beans."

"Stop worrying," said Sam. "Look, last time I came back, so why wouldn't it happen again?"

Splodge tried explaining about invisibility, but it was no use, Sam was far too excited, working out the best combination for frightening the pants off Hilda Hardbottom.

"Hi," he said calmly, walking into the kitchen for tea. "I am so hungry I am almost fading away."

Ernie and Hilda nearly jumped out of their skins when they saw a cap and a pair of trousers coming towards them.

"I don't think this is right, dearest," said Ernie, dropping the newspaper. "Shouldn't we be able to see him?"

"Of course we should," said Hilda shakily.

"I think it might be best to take him home, and get a doctor to have a look at him," said Ernie.

"What do you think would happen, you ninny, if we went home with an invisible boy?" said Hilda,

"I don't know, sweetpea," said Ernie.

Hilda sat down at the kitchen table. She was really worried. This wasn't in her grand plan. In fact she could be accused of causing Sam's disappearance. Then they would be in deep trouble. Hilda couldn't allow her plan to go wrong, not now when she was so close to getting what she wanted. Maureen Cook from Dream Maker Tours had said it was only a matter of her seeing Sam, then the money would be as good as theirs.

"Remember the ear, sweetpea, it came back," said Ernie, trying to sound encouraging.

Hilda filled their bowls with green slimy pea soup.

"Eat up," she said, putting on her TV face, "we don't want you fading away altogether now, do we."

Sam took off his cap and put it on the table. Hilda jumped back. There was now nothing to show that Sam was sitting in his seat, except a spoon playing with the slimy soup.

"I don't much like pea soup," said Sam, who was enjoying seeing Hilda squirm.

"What do you like?" said Hilda nervously. "You can have anything you want as long as it helps make you visible again."

So Sam gave her a long list, starting with twelve small bottles of tomato ketchup.

17

That night Hilda couldn't sleep. She was walking up and down in the lounge when a picture came off the wall right in front of her, and a china dog started to move across the mantelpiece. Sam was having fun.

"Is that you, Sam?" she said in a shaky voice. Sam didn't answer. Splodge, who was also invisible, was tickling her leg. She let out a scream and Ernie came in, yawning. What he saw made his legs wobbly with fright. A chair was floating round the room.

"That's not right," said Ernie, "I mean, chairs don't do that, do they?"

The chair dropped to the ground with a thud.

"Of course they don't, you ninny," Hilda said trembling.

"You know, sweetpea," said Ernie, "I think this place might be haunted. I just felt a rush of cold air." The lounge door closed with a bang.

Hilda recovered herself. "Of course it's not haunted," she snapped, picking up a cushion and hitting out at thin air. "Take that, you little toerag," she shouted. But Sam and Splodge had left, and were safely out of the way in the shed.

"I like being invisible," said Sam. "The only drawback is that it's chilly without your clothes on."

"Pish bosh, you're supposed to come and go, not stay like that all the time," said Splodge. "The sooner we get a message home the better."

The CB radio was not working that well, mainly because it had been wired to the receiver the wrong way. It took

Splodge some time to get it sorted out.

"Come on," said Sam, "I'm getting chilly out here."

"Well go back to the monster grotto then," said Splodge, "and make us something to fill up gurgling tummy."

The radio was now making strange noises and Splodge kept moving the knobs and listening. Then he started speaking in a language that Sam couldn't understand.

"Χαλλινγ Πλανεντ τεν ρινγσ"

Sam walked back towards the bungalow. The lounge looked as if a giant hippo had had hysterics. Hilda had finally gone to bed exhausted, and was snoring like a battleship attacking her enemy.

The great thing about being invisible, thought Sam, opening the fridge and looking inside, is that I don't feel frightened any more. I have some power and that is a truly wicked feeling. He poured out all the milk there was into two glasses, made a pile of peanut butter sandwiches and found the last bottle of tomato ketchup.

"I've got message home," said Splodge, becoming visible again. "They've heard of a sick grotter, in fact it's caused quite a hollerburluke. Something is definitely stuck inside it. They're on their way out to it. Also my mum says not to worry and sends you her toodle hyes."

"Oh that's wonderful," said Sam. "So what will happen now?"

"Mum and Dad want to say hi and talk to me again tomorrow. Also I've got to tell them about the invisible problem," mumbled Splodge. "I'm sure my dad and mum can think of something."

18

The bungalow was unusually quiet the next morning. Hilda had taken the car into the village to do some shopping, and Ernie was in the shed, playing with his radio. To his delight it was working better than it had ever done before, picking up some very strange sounds, "Χαλλινγ σπλογε σπαχε σηυττλε ρχοϖερεδ αλλ ον βοαρδ αρε σαφε."

Sam and Splodge spent the best part of the morning in the lounge. Sam was still invisible, but today he was dressed. It was too chilly to walk about without your clothes on. They sat together on the beaten up sofa, eating cereal out of the packet, watching whatever they wanted on TV.

Ernie, who had been left with strict instructions not to let Sam out of his sight, kept coming in from the shed, and saying, "You all right then?" On one of these visits he was sure he saw a green spotty little fellow sitting next to Sam, but then again he might just be seeing things, he hadn't got his glasses on, and the next time he looked it had gone.

About two o'clock the phone rang. Ernie picked it up. It was Maureen Cook from Dream Maker Tours. She couldn't have sounded more helpful, and said she would be coming down to see Sam tomorrow, to talk about his future.

"That will be nice," said Ernie, putting down the phone and telling Sam what she had just said.

"Do you think she will recognise me?" asked Sam.

"Oh dear," said Ernie. "Oh dear, I forgot you were invisible."

Hilda was not in a good mood when she arrived home at teatime, weighed down by shopping bags. Her mood was not improved one little bit when Ernie told her about Maureen Cook. She started rumbling like an old boiler ready to burst.

"You are worse than hopeless, you peabrain," she said to Ernie, who was looking very sheepish. "What are we going to show her, an invisible boy?"

"Perhaps," said Sam, "if you were kind to me, I might become visible again."

"It's worth a try," said Ernie in a small shaky voice.

Hilda said nothing, but banged and thumped round the kitchen unpacking the shopping.

"Oh that looks nice, sweetpea," said Ernie, seeing all the things Sam had asked for, including the twelve bottles of tomato ketchup.

"Well, none of it's for you," she snapped at Ernie. "It isn't you that's invisible, more's the pity." She handed Sam a bag. "Put these on," she ordered.

In it were a woolly balaclava, a pair of multi-coloured gloves, a cheap pair of dark glasses, and as the finishing touch, a pair of plastic joke lips.

"What are these for?" said Sam, laughing.

"This isn't funny," said Hilda. "Just do as I say."

When he saw himself in the hall mirror he couldn't stop laughing. Oh, now he really did look scary, as if he were about to rob a bank. Roll on tomorrow, he thought. How was Hilda going to get out of this mess?

19

The reason, Splodge said, that Splodgerdites adored tomato ketchup was simple. It was the sauce of their good looks, it kept them young, healthy, and wise. Also,

 growing tomatoes was unheard of on Planet Ten Rings. It was only on earth that the tomato could be transformed into the right stuff for aliens.

"Have you been here lots of times, then?" asked Sam.

Splodge looked down at his toes. "No," he said, "I have only been here once before with my dad, and it was a short sort of visit."

It turned out that Splodge was only about as old as Sam, and that this was the first time he had travelled on his own to earth.

"I thought I would get my mum a present," said Splodge sadly, "but it all went a bit starshaped. I am only a junior space flyer, I start my AST course next year."

"What's that?" asked Sam.

"Advanced Space Travel," said Splodge. "That's when we learn everything to do with space and all the other things like grotters and orgbacks."

Sam didn't like to ask, he had a nasty feeling he already knew the answer.

"Have you ever used one of those invisible patches before?" he said.

"No," said Splodge.

"Do you know what happens when one of those patches is put on a boy like me?" asked Sam.

"No," said Splodge, looking a little shamefaced. "They are only to be used when everything is whamdangled."

Sam was beginning to feel panicky. It was one thing to be invisible for a few days, but not forever. What if his parents came back? How would they know it was Sam if they couldn't see him?

"Will I ever be visible again?" asked Sam anxiously.

"Need to speak to Dad," said Splodge. "I'm sure someone on Ten Rings will know what to do."

But it was proving to be quite difficult to get a message home. Ernie had been fiddling again with the radio and it took Splodge ages to pick up a signal, and then he could hardly hear what they were saying, except for the odd word like σουνδ σηυττλε σαφε.

"We'll have to try again tomorrow," said Sam, seeing the look on Splodge's face. He was tired and his bright green skin was losing its shine.

"Pish bosh, I want to go home," he said sadly. "I miss my mum."

"I know," said Sam. He took Splodge back to the house, gave him a bottle of tomato ketchup and tucked him up in bed.

"So do I," said Sam quietly. "I miss Mum and Dad very much indeed."

20

The next day the Hardbottoms were up early, cleaning and tidying the bungalow.

Hilda put on her smiling face that she kept at the bottom of an old make-up bag and only used for special occasions. Ernie put on his one and only suit. The tea had been set out on a tray in the lounge, and the curtains were drawn. Hilda had put

Sam in the armchair with a rug over his knees. When Ernie saw him sitting there in the balaclava and dark glasses and false lips, he jumped with fright.

"Hilda," he said, "there's a strange man sitting in the armchair.

He wasn't there a moment ago. Did you let him in? He looks very scarey!"

"That, you peabrain, is Sam," said Hilda.

When Maureen Cook arrived she was rather taken aback by the Hardbottoms' idea of a holiday. The bungalow was seedy, and smelt damp.

"You could have taken yourselves somewhere nice and hot," she said. "We would happily have paid."

"Didn't want to look too greedy," said Hilda, smiling. "Not until all this is settled, so to speak."

"Please remember," said Maureen, "Dream Maker Tours are here to make your dreams a reality."

"I hope so," said Hilda, taking Maureen through to the lounge, and placing her in the chair furthest away from Sam. Hilda handed her a cup of tea and a piece of cake, talking all the time, like a car alarm that wouldn't stop, about how much they cared for Sam and how he enjoyed sitting in the dark wearing a balaclava.

"It makes him feel protected from the outside world. Grief," said Hilda, "can do strange things to one."

"Please Mrs Hardbottom," said Maureen, "will you let me speak. Are you feeling all right, Sam?" she asked.

"As I said," interrupted Hilda, "Sam is a bit shy."

Sam nodded and mumbled, "I'm OK."

"Do you like it here?" Maureen started.

Hilda interrupted again. "These questions aren't too strenuous, are they?" she said, sounding concerned. "It's just that we care so much for the boy, and want to protect him. After all, I'm not called the Nation's Favourite Neighbour for nothing."

"Quite so," said Maureen, bringing a picture of Sam out of her briefcase, and going over to the window to draw back the curtains. "I would like to see your face,

Sam, if you don't mind."

"I do mind," said Hilda, rushing past her and standing in front of the window. "He has been through an awful lot, why does he have to answer these questions? Isn't it enough that he's here?"

"I am just doing my job, Mrs Hardbottom," said Maureen wearily. This wasn't going to plan. She had hoped to have all this sorted out in no time at all.

"Treacle toffee," said Hilda, holding out a sweet tin. "I made it myself."

Maureen smiled weakly. "Well, one piece if you insist, then I must ask Sam these questions."

Sam watched the look of horror spread over Maureen Cook's face as her jaws slowly stuck together and she was unable to say another word.

Hilda took her back to the chair farthest away from Sam.

"Shall we talk about the money?" said Hilda, smiling charmingly.

At that moment Ernie came into the room. "Wonderful news, sweetpea," he said. "The Star shuttle has made contact with Earth. I just heard it on my CB radio. It looks like Mr and Mrs Ray will be coming home after all."

"Hooray!" shouted Sam, sending the false pair of lips shooting across the room.

Maureen looked startled and Sam put his gloved hand across his mouth and said, "It's the best bit of news ever."

21

Maureen Cook had written out a cheque to cover their holiday expenses.

"Is that all?" said Hilda, seeing how little she had been given.

But Maureen was now running towards her car, still unable to speak, a hanky held over her mouth.

"Wait a minute, come back," shouted Hilda.

It was too late. Maureen sped off down the road at top speed.

"It's all your fault," Hilda screamed at Ernie. "If you hadn't come charging in like that, we would have been given loads of money."

Hilda marched like an invading army into the shed. She got hold of the CB radio, and lifted it high above her head.

"Don't do that!" shouted Ernie and Sam together. It was too late. Hilda threw it to the ground.

"I think," said Ernie sadly, "you've gone and broken it."

"I hope so," said Hilda. "If you had half a brain, you would have seen what I was trying to do instead of mucking up all my plans."

Hilda went back into the kitchen followed by Sam. All that could be seen of him now was a pair of dark glasses.

"You wretched boy, none of this would have happened if you hadn't gone invisible," yelled Hilda. "Well, you can stop playing games. I haven't come this far for you to ruin everything. You are going to become visible again and tell your mum and dad you had a lovely time with us.

Do you hear me?"

Sam, who had long lost his fear of
Hilda, said calmly, "I won't. I will tell them
the truth, that you are a mean, nasty two-
faced witch."

Hilda grabbed a broom. "What did you
call me?" she shouted, bringing it down
with a nasty crack on the sunglasses,
which fell broken to the floor.

At that moment Splodge walked
into the room, quite visible.

"I agree," he said.

Hilda dropped her
broom and scrambled up
on the table as fast as her
tubby legs would let her.
Splodge went over to
where the broken glasses
lay, and picked them up.

"You," said Splodge, "should be boggled."

Hilda started screaming at the top of her voice.

Ernie came in holding his smashed radio.

"Look!" yelled Hilda, pointing at Splodge. "It's a monster, a rat, an alien. Don't stand there, do something!"

If Ernie wasn't mistaken, this was the same little fellow that he had seen sitting with Sam the other day on the sofa.

"Well, what are you waiting for? I think that creature has murdered Sam!" said Hilda "Look at the smashed glasses."

Ernie said nothing. He had seen many frightening things in his life, though sadly none of them as frightening as his wife when she was in one of her moods.

"I can't see what all the fuss is about," said Sam, invisible from the other side of the room. "That's my friend Splodge, from Planet Ten Rings, and he's not best pleased that you have ruined his spaceship by filling it with water."

Hilda went white with fright. "Do something, Ernie," she pleaded.

For the first time since he had married Hilda, way back in the dark ages, Ernie felt brave. If a boy and a little alien could stand up to her, so could he.

"No, I won't," he said firmly. "You have gone too far this time, Hilda. I should have had the courage to stop you, but I didn't – more's the pity."

Splodge stepped forward. "You are a cruel and mean hard bottom, and you give earth H beans a bad name," he said, holding his little hands out before him. Bright green rays came out of his fingertips. Hilda's face went a horrid pink and then became covered in tiny green spots.

"Nice one," said Sam.

Hilda quickly climbed down off the table, ran into the hall, grabbed her coat and hat, stuffed the cheque into her handbag and ran out of the front door and down the street as fast as her stumpy legs would carry her.

22

On the TV that night, every programme was about the Star Shuttle's miraculous return to earth. Experts were talking about black holes and all sort of other theories to explain how a spaceship could go missing for so long. No one mentioned grotters or a small planet called Ten Rings.

Splodge had been spending the evening trying to wire the radio up to his spaceship in the hope of getting a message home, but it wasn't working. Ernie was out in the back yard with the receiver.

"Try it now," said Ernie.

There were a few beeping noises and then nothing.

"Pish bosh, it's hopeless," said Splodge sadly. "We are truly boggled."

"Often when things don't work," said Sam "my dad gives them a little tap. He says it helps them wake up."

"Go on then," said Splodge.

Sam tapped the top of the spaceship. Nothing happened.

"Well," said Splodge, "it doesn't work."

But that was as far as he got. The spaceship suddenly lit up. Sparks of rainbow colour came shooting out of it, lighting up the drab back yard.

"OW!" said Sam.

Then they all heard

Τηισ ισ πλανεντ τεν Ρινγσ Χαλλινγ Σπλοδγε

"That's my dad!" shouted Splodge. "That's my dad!"

It was a much larger spacecraft that landed in the back yard that night, and Splodge's parents were thrilled to see their son.

"This is Sam," said Splodge, looking down at his toes. Sam held out the arm of his old jumper.

"Oh dear," said Splodge's dad. "What have you done, junior?"

"He was trying to protect me," said Sam.

"He didn't realise I couldn't go invisible."

"Sorry, Dad," said Splodge.

His dad smiled a kind smile. "Well, we'd better put it right."

He held out his hands and a blue light flashed around Sam. The next thing, there he was, visible again.

"Thank you," said Sam. "Oh, it's great to be seen again."

Ernie offered to make them tea, but Splodge's parents wanted to get home as soon as possible.

"Wait a minute, I can't go without Mum's present," said Splodge.

He rushed back into the bungalow and brought out twelve bottles of tomato ketchup.

"These are for you, Mum," said Splodge.

She gave him a hug, then thanked Sam for looking after him so well. "He's a bit young to be doing this," she said, waving goodbye. Sam wanted to thank Splodge's parents for helping him find his mum and dad, but there was no time. He was interrupted by the noise of police cars screeching down the road. Splodge just had time to wave before the doors of the spaceship closed behind him. Then there was a whirling noise and in a shower of lights and glitter they were gone.

The police were now knocking loudly on the front door. "Mr and Mrs Hardbottom," they shouted, "open up in the name of the law."

23

It was the best homecoming ever. Mum and Dad were over the moon to see their beloved boy. They couldn't have been more proud of Sam, and how well he had coped under such appalling circumstances. It was hard to believe that Hilda could have turned out to be so cruel and horrible.

It had been Maureen Cook who had alerted the police. They had arrived just in time to see sparks coming from behind the garden wall.

They had driven Sam home in style to his parents, the blue lights flashing all the way to 2 Plunket Road.

Ernie had been taken away for questioning, while Hilda was caught trying to get on a flight for Majorca. It was her pink face with its green spots that had given her away.

Mr and Mrs Hardbottom were both charged with abduction and trying to take money under false pretences.

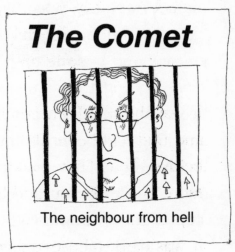

The Comet

The neighbour from hell

Hilda had at last found the fame she had been looking for. Her picture appeared on every newspaper, with the caption "The neighbour from hell." She was sent to prison. Ernie was let off with a caution. The judge felt that if he hadn't been so frightened of his wife he wouldn't have gone along with her plan.

Mum and Dad felt relieved that it was all over, and they were just happy to be back on earth with Sam.

The funny thing was they had no memory at all of what happened to them, except of falling asleep on the homeward journey and waking up again as they were landing. Everyone on board had been most surprised to find out that anything had been wrong, or that they had been missing for so long. Even the officials at Houston agreed that the space shuttle disappearance was a mystery.

"It's like it became invisible," said one Houston scientist.

Sam kept quiet about Splodge. Who would believe him? At her trial Hilda had gone on about aliens, and how boys couldn't be seen, only heard. Everyone thought she had gone barmy.

After it was all over, Ernie lived quietly next door, pottering in his garden. One evening while Sam was kicking a football round, Ernie leaned over the fence and said to him, "There's something that really bothers me."

"What?" said Sam.

"That little fellow Splodge, he asked me something as I was helping him with the radio. He said did I know the meaning of 57 varieties? Do you think," said Ernie, "that he was talking about space and the universe?"

"Tomato ketchup," said Sam.

Ernie looked puzzled.

"That's what it says on the ketchup bottle, 57 varieties," said Sam, and they both burst out laughing.

More Stories

The Strongest Girl in the World

Josie Jenkins, aged eight and three quarters, is good at doing tricks, but she amazes herself and everyone else with her strength when she lifts a table, a car, and even a bus with no effort at all. Mr Two Suit promises to bring her fame and fortune – and so he does. But when Josie and her mum and dad and brother Louis are flown to New York and she becomes a celebrity, she finds that she has to cope with all kinds of ups and downs.

The Smallest Girl Ever

Everyone expects Ruby Genie to have the same fantastic magical powers as her famous parents did. But Ruby can't do any magic at all. Or so she thinks. Then Ruby begins to get smaller... and smaller. And she discovers that even though she is so tiny she can fit into a handbag, she can still be clever and brave and find people to love her.

The Boy Who Could Fly

One day the Fat Fairy turns up at Thomas Top's house to grant him a birthday wish. Thomas can't think what to ask for, so he wishes he could fly. That's how Thomas goes from being just an ordinary boy whom no one notices to being the most popular boy in the school. But it makes him sad that grown-ups can't see the wonderful things he can do – especially his dad.

The Boy with the Magic Numbers

When Billy Pickles' dad leaves home to live in New York, he gives Billy a moneybox. Billy's not sure where to put in the money, and not sure why his dad has left.

When Billy goes to New York to visit his father and his Italian grandmother, he discovers the secret of his magic moneybox at last. In a wonderful adventure, he takes Mighty Mamma on a helicopter ride, cracks open a safe, solves a kidnap mystery – and gets to know his dad again.